Life of the Party

'It was okay,' said Steph. 'Up to a point.'

Which meant, *I was enjoying it till you spoilt it, Chloe*. I felt rotten and I knew when I was sober I was going to feel even rottener.

'Never again,' I mumbled. 'Honest, Steph, I'll never touch another drop.'

She took my arm, and gratefully I leaned into it.

'I've heard that one before,' she said.

But at least she laughed.

Look out for other exciting stories
in the *Shades* series:

A Murder of Crows by Penny Bates
Blitz by David Orme
Cry, Baby by Jill Atkins
Cuts Deep by Catherine Johnson
Danger Money by Mary Chapman
Doing the Double by Alan Durant
Fighting Back by Helen Bird
Fire! by David Orme
Four Degrees More by Malcolm Rose
Gateway from Hell by John Banks
Hunter's Moon by John Townsend
Nightmare Park by Philip Preece
Mantrap by Tish Farrell
Plague by David Orme
Shouting at the Stars by David Belbin
Space Explorers by David Johnson
Tears of a Friend by Joanna Kenrick
The Messenger by John Townsend
Treachery by Night by Ann Ruffell
Virus by Mary Chapman
Who Cares? by Helen Bird
Witness by Anne Cassidy

Life of the Party

Gillian Philip

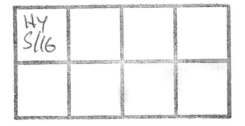

HY
S/16

Evans

Published by Evans Brothers Limited
2A Portman Mansions
Chiltern St
London W1U 6NR

British Library Cataloguing in Publication Data
Philip, Gillian
    Life of the party. - (Shades)
    1. Binge drinking - Fiction 2. Drunk driving -
Fiction
    3. Young adult fiction
    I. Title
    823.9'2[J]

ISBN-13: 9780237534974

Editor: Julia Moffatt
Designer: Rob Walster

Chapter One

'What have I got?' I yelled. 'Two heads?'

Steph snorted with laughter, but the boy who was staring didn't seem to think it was funny. Rob Yeadon, the jerk.

This was the best thing in my changed life: I wasn't shy any more. Not scared to speak my mind. I didn't hold back my opinions, or a snappy retort. Flipping the top off another Breezer, I giggled. Two heads! Good line! I liked that.

'Sometimes I wonder,' said Rob Yeadon. 'Half a brain in each, like?'

'Ignore him,' said Steph. She glared at Rob.

Good old Steph. My best friend. It was Steph who'd befriended me, given me confidence. Before Steph, I'd thought I wasn't worth knowing.

I wasn't. Even my own father used to phone Mum with some excuse, the night before I was due to spend the weekend with him. He was still sorting out his life, he said. He needed space. Well, if even my dad tried to get out of my company, why would anyone else want it?

Except that Steph did. And instead of feeling sorry for me, she got angry at Dad. *He* was the selfish one, she used to say. *He* was the one who didn't deserve *me*. And after laughing nervously a few times, and shrugging, I'd started to believe her. Yeah, she was right. It wasn't all my fault. I wasn't a worthless human being. I was entitled to some fun, too, and a life.

Yeah, she'd say. *Dead right, Chloe! Forget him, and forget that Rob Yeadon and all.*

Steph had cottoned on straight away that I fancied Rob but was too shy to do anything about it. Anyway, if he wasn't looking at me like something the cat dragged in, he was ignoring me. *He's obnoxious*. Steph would tease me, cheer me up. *Come on, have a drink.*

If I was mad or miserable, I could call her and she'd talk sense into me and make me laugh. We always had a laugh.

Even Steph could be a pain, though. Even Steph sometimes dragged me down. Like now.

'You're never having another?' Her

eyebrows were practically up in her hairline.

'Like you've been a model of sobriety all night!' I laughed.

'Yeah. I didn't start at four o'clock, though.'

I wondered if Steph was one of those people who needed a tame sidekick, a stooge to boss around. Suspicion made me suddenly, blazingly angry.

'Have you got a problem?' I snapped.

She looked bewildered, and even a bit hurt.

'I've got a mind of my own, you know,' I spat. 'Have you got a problem with that?'

Her puzzlement turned to cold fury. She stood up very abruptly.

'I think it's you that's got the problem, Chloe.' Snatching up her half-empty plastic cup – and almost spilling it – she stormed off.

I felt really pleased with myself. My mind

sharp and keen, my head light, I was on top of the world. I'd shown them all: Rob Yeadon and that up-herself cow Steph as well. Oh sure, she made me laugh and gave me confidence, but so did alcohol. I wasn't dependent on her. I wasn't dependent on anyone but myself.

And then I saw the stupid little smile on Rob Yeadon's face. He was standing in a dark corner of the room with a couple of his thick pals, eyeing up the girls. Except at that moment he wasn't. He'd obviously just said something to his mate, who looked straight at me and laughed. And Rob Yeadon just stared at me again and shook his head and smiled.

He was laughing at me. Laughing at me!

All the good feeling drained out through the soles of my feet, which made me feel dizzy again, but not in a nice way. My stomach felt cold as I realised what I'd said to Steph. Straight away I forgot it again, but whatever it was, it made my head spin horribly. The music in here was way too loud. My brain throbbed, which wasn't nice in a spinning head. Automatically I lifted the bottle to my lips, but now it tasted too sweet, like sugary chemicals. My throat lifted.

Oh, boy, did my throat lift. Somehow I got to my feet and bolted for the flat door. Luckily it was a ground floor flat; I'd never have made it down the stairs.

Steph caught up with me in the narrow close alongside the flats. I'd been sick out in the street as well – luckily there weren't many people around – and then I'd limped into the alleyway and been sick again. Several times. I hated being sick but at least it made me feel a bit better.

I leaned on the wall with both hands. It

was a nice wall. I liked the coolness of the stone against my palms. So I put my forehead against it as well.

Steph rubbed my back.

'You okay?' she asked gently.

I thought I was going to say something intelligent, but instead I just groaned.

'Poor old you,' she said.

Which was more sympathy than I deserved.

'I'm really sorry, Steph,' I managed to say.

'Don't worry about it, kiddo. Come on, I'll get you home.'

'But you wanted to—'

'Have you any idea how late it is? C'mon, it's time to go anyway. It was getting boring.'

And so were you, Chloe. But she was too kind to say it.

'Sorry,' I said again. Experimentally I

pushed myself away from the wall. I swayed, but I could walk roughly in a straight line.

'Whose flat was that, anyway?'

She shrugged. 'Dunno. Some mate of Martin's big brother.'

I was really glad I didn't know the flat owner. I sort of suspected how embarrassed I was going to be in the morning.

'Was it a good party?'

'It was okay,' said Steph. 'Up to a point.'

Which meant, *I was enjoying it till you spoilt it, Chloe.* I felt rotten and I knew when I was sober I was going to feel even rottener.

'Never again,' I mumbled. 'Honest, Steph, I'll never touch another drop.'

She took my arm, and gratefully I leaned into it.

'I've heard that one before,' she said.

But at least she laughed.

It was especially kind of Steph not to dump me at my front door and run. Instead she took my keys out of my bag and got me inside, and stayed beside me to face the wrath of Mum.

Not that Mum's wrath amounted to much.

'Oh, Chloe, for goodness' sake.' She put her hand to her mouth. She was in the hallway, in her dressing gown, and she looked dazed, as if she'd been asleep but had heard us coming. That wouldn't have been difficult, since I'd fallen over when I opened the gate, and knocked over the wheelie bin.

'It's okay, Mrs Finch,' said Steph firmly. 'Really it is. Chloe just doesn't feel too good.'

'Don't feel too good,' I muttered.

'So I'll just get her up to her room…'

'Chloe.' There were tears in Mum's voice. 'Was it something that happened? Is it me

13

and Dad? Is there something I can…'

Even feeling as bad as I did, I could still give her a withering glare. No, it was nothing you did, I wanted to say. No, I'm hardly going to be bothered about Dad when he's not bothered about me. All I'm doing is having a good time. Don't be so understanding and – *patronising*.

I couldn't be bothered saying anything. But I think she got the point of the glare.

'Tomorrow,' she said lamely. 'We'll talk about this tomorrow. Right, love?'

Tomorrow, I thought, I'd better avoid Mum like the plague.

Avoiding Mum was easy enough; she was annoyed with me, that was for sure, but she was also dreading the confrontation, and she's no better in the mornings than I am. She muttered something over breakfast about *talking later*, then scurried off to work.

I wish I could have avoided Rob Yeadon as easily.

He grinned at me as he came into the classroom, a superior sort of grin. I was sitting at my desk, hoping I wasn't going to have to stand up any time soon, because I felt nauseous again. He leaned down as he passed, specially to insult me.

'Looking rough,' he murmured.

'Yeah, you are that,' I snapped.

If I'd had a drink inside me, I could have thought of something wittier. But that would have to do.

He was like a bad virus. He wouldn't go away.

'To think I used to fancy you,' he sneered. 'Before you were such a cheap drunk.'

That took my breath away. Even if I'd thought of a snappy retort I couldn't have got it out. I stared at the pile of books on my desk, trying not to be sick, and feeling desperately hurt. *Might have told me earlier*, was all I could think.

Talk about irony.

Might have told me, when I was too shy and insecure to tell *him*. Might have told me, maybe, before I started drinking more so I'd have the confidence to chat him up…

Oh, sod him. I had friends. Plenty of friends. I was the life and soul of the party these days.

Best of all I had Steph. I leaned across to her.

'The park later?'

She grinned. 'Thought you were staying in for the rest of your life?'

'I need some fresh air,' I hissed, jerking my head at Rob Yeadon.

'Been having a go at you? Ignore him.'

She sniffed. 'Yeah, okay. Meet you after tea?'

'Great!'

I wanted some company. I hated that nagging voice that had crept back into my brain, the one that said I was ugly and worthless and pointless. I just wanted to hang out with friends who liked me.

It wasn't as if I was going to have a drink or anything.

Chapter Two

'You're dead funny, you. You're a good laugh.'

Wished I could say the same about Kieran. He was Ricky Browning's older brother, and he was sitting way too close to me on the picnic table, resting his feet on the bench. The sun had sunk beyond the tops of the trees, the picnic area was in

shadow, and it was definitely getting cooler.
I hoped Kieran wasn't going to offer to
warm me up.

Supposedly, drink makes boys look better.
For me it was working the other way round.
An hour ago I'd thought Kieran was kind of
cute. Now he was trying to snuggle up, I
could see his lips were flabby, his eyes leery,
and he had a zit on the side of his nose.
Most likely so did I, and probably Rob
Yeadon did too, but there was something
dead off-putting about Kieran's.

I wished Rob Yeadon wouldn't keep
barging into my thoughts. I took a swig of
cider to fend him off.

I'd be fending off Kieran in a minute. I just
knew he'd try and kiss me soon and then I'd
be sick. I felt queasy enough already, like last
night was catching up with me again. So I
kept making cutting remarks to try and put

him off, but he just kept chortling.

'You're a scream, Chloe!'

No, I just felt like screaming...

I craned my head round to try and talk to Ricky, who was nearest. I quite liked Ricky, who was in our class and was better-looking than his brother and less of a pain in the neck, but he was hardly worth talking to right now, since he had his tongue halfway down Jenna's throat. Didn't exactly make Jenna scintillating company either.

Steph wasn't helping. Ricky's mate Calum was chatting her up, and she wasn't paying attention to me, and I was getting more annoyed by the second. I took another swig from the plastic cider bottle. That felt a bit better.

Thoughtfully I studied the bottle. For goodness' sake. That couldn't have been me. Could it? I couldn't have knocked that back all by myself…

Trouble was, I was bored. Bored, and there was nothing to do but keep taking mouthfuls of cider. I was fed up with the lot of them, and the worst of it was I couldn't just go home.

At least it was a beautiful evening. The sky was bright blue, the tips of the pine trees still gilded with light. The rickety picnic table was way out of town in the armpit of nowhere – well, beside the forest walk car park four miles out of town – and we'd come here because we'd had enough of the municipal park. Too many kids running around screaming their heads off.

There wasn't any peace, and some jerk in a blue anorak moaned about us sitting on the swings, and even though Ricky swore at him in technicolour, he wouldn't leave us alone. In the end it had been easier to take our carry-out somewhere else. Kieran had a car, so we all squeezed in, shrieking and giggling, and drove out here to the forest.

Which had been fine when we were still having fun. But I didn't feel too good, and now I just wanted to go home. I wished Steph would snog Calum and get it over with.

The more I thought about it the angrier I got. She should have guessed I was feeling rough. She knew I'd been sick last night. And again this morning, in the toilets at break time.

I was the party girl around here. I couldn't be the one to say it was time to go. I needed Steph to back me up. I needed Steph, full stop, but she was all wrapped up in some boy…

I took another swig.

'Hey, kiddo!'

I must have been in a daze, because

Steph was suddenly in front of me, grinning, Calum's arm around her waist. Kieran's arm was around mine, for that matter, and his hand was sneaking higher. Shuddering, I slapped it away, and yanked his arm off me.

'Oy, what's your problem?' Kieran muttered a curse and jumped down off the table to rummage in the off-licence bag.

'Yeah, what's wrong?' Steph frowned – perhaps because I was scowling at her – and I saw her glance quickly at my two-litre bottle. She grinned again.

'Is that your *second?*'

I stared at it, and at her.

'No. Anyway, there's nothing else to do around here.'

I kicked the first, empty bottle with my heel so it rolled down under the wooden table.

'You were the one who wanted to come,'

she pointed out.

'Yeah, well, that was before everybody decided to ignore me.'

'Who's ignoring you?' she snapped. 'I'm just talking to Calum.'

I gave her a scathing look, jumped down off the table and marched towards the woods.

Steph followed me. I could tell she was about to lose her temper. Well, good. About time she realised there was someone else in the world besides Calum.

'I thought you were getting on fine with Kieran. You were practically sitting on his lap in the car. You weren't bothered then.'

'Yeah,' I blustered, ' 'cause there were six people in the car. Where else was I going to sit? He's been pawing me for ages and I can't stand him. I want to go home.'

Steph grabbed my arm to slow me down.

'Look, what's wrong? We're all having a good time. I *thought* we were having a good time. Come on, it's a laugh.'

'Not much of a laugh for me. Just because you can't take your hands off Calum.'

She stopped abruptly and yanked on my arm so that I had to stop too. It hurt.

'What are we, joined at the hip? Can't I talk to anyone else? I really like Calum, you know that.'

'Yeah, but I'm supposed to be your friend and you're ignoring me.'

'No I'm *not*.' She glowered at me. 'Don't be so selfish. Are you really going to break up the party just because you're in a strop?'

Shaking her off I stepped back, too angry to cry. The trouble was, I knew I was being unreasonable. She was talking to me again, wasn't she?

I just wasn't that keen on what she

was saying.

The trees around me wouldn't stay still; they kept shifting ever so slightly, like my eyeballs were sliding around in my head, and the effect made me dizzy. I gripped a tree trunk to stop me grabbing Steph. After all, I didn't need her.

'There's no party to break up. This is crap.'

She took a long deep breath.

'Listen, let's not get mad at each other.'

'No, don't get mad, cause I'm not going to spoil anybody's fun. Right?'

I had a nasty feeling I was starting to slur my words. I really didn't think it was me who had started the second bottle but I'd certainly drunk out of it. And was it really the second or the third? How had that happened?

At least I'd stopped feeling queasy. A hair of the dog, they called it. Just a tiny bit

more alcohol to balance your system.
Feeling a little tipsy beat feeling as rotten as
I'd felt this morning. When Rob Yeadon
called me a cheap drunk…

Tears stung my eyes.

'I'm going,' I said.

'Wait.' Steph almost grabbed me again,
but restrained herself. 'I'll go and get—'

'No!' I yelled. 'I'm not getting back in
that idiot's car. I'll walk!'

Kieran reddened with rage, pointing a
bottle at me.

'Dead right! No way is she getting back
in my car! The little cow can walk!'

Whoops. I hadn't meant him to hear.
Looked like I'd burned my bridges, but so
what?

'I wasn't going to get Kieran or anybody
else,' said Steph narkily. 'I was going to get
my bag. I'll come with you.'

'Don't bother.' I really did feel guilty now, but I snapped at her anyway. I felt guilty, and miserable, and if I didn't go now I was going to burst into self-pitying tears in front of them all. 'I don't need company.'

'Yeah you do. Look, forget that stupid jerk Yeadon. He's not worth it.'

Yeah, but all I could think was *I used to fancy you, Chloe, before you were a cheap drunk...*

'You can do better than him. Come on, lighten up.' Steph gave me a conciliatory grin.

'Quit patronising me,' I hissed. 'I'm going home. I'll see you tomorrow.'

'You can't walk all that way on your own. I'm coming with you.'

'You are not. Stay with your pal Calum.'

'Never mind Calum. There's no way you can walk.' She sounded genuinely anxious.

'It's too far and it'll be dark soon. I'll come with you.'

'See? You're doing it again. I am *fine*. I don't need you, right?'

I was really losing my temper now. After all, she was as good as calling me a useless drunk. Funny coming from her, when she could tank it back with the best of them. Who was she to pass judgement on Rob Yeadon, anyway? Maybe she was jealous. Maybe she even fancied him herself.

You know, even at that moment I knew I was being irrational. Trouble was, I didn't care. I was speaking my mind. It was a mind of my own, and I was proud of it.

'I can look after myself!' I yelled, turning on my heel.

'Chloe, what do you think you—'

Hadn't I made myself clear enough, or what?

'Don't follow me!' I screamed. 'I'm fed up with you, okay? I *don't need you*, and I *don't want your company*. Is that getting through yet?'

'Oh yes,' she called bitterly after me, 'that's got through. Get over yourself, Chloe!'

I was already blinking back tears as I stormed off towards the main road, but she went ahead and made it a lot worse. I heard her footsteps running after me, then she stopped and called, a bit more gently, 'Be careful, kiddo. Okay? See you tomorrow.'

Kiddo. *Kiddo*. That just about summed her up. Treating me like her baby sister instead of her best friend. Furiously I rubbed tears off my face. I was doing my best to stay angry, but it really was a long way home. I was walking off the edge of the alcohol, and the late evening air hurt my brain, and I was starting to realise how badly I'd overreacted.

However hard I tried to remember why I'd got so angry, I just couldn't. Yet it had seemed really important at the time and it had been so clear. Steph used me and patronised me. Didn't she? Yes. No. Yes. I tried not to think. I tried to use all my energy staying furious.

Trouble was, I was using up so much of it sobbing and snivelling.

It was getting dark, and it was a lot colder now. I wasn't wearing a jacket, just a thin camisole top and a useless little fashion-scarf. My feet hurt along with the rest of me. Cars swept past, and I told myself I was only imagining that some of the drivers slowed and stared as they went by. When I limped to the outskirts of town I just about fainted with relief, till I remembered I still had a couple of miles to walk home.

At least by the time I got there I was too footsore and miserable to worry any more about my disastrous evening. Though it was after midnight, I knew Mum was awake – I could see the light under her door, hear the rustle of the magazine she was pretending to read – but I didn't go in to say goodnight. I didn't want any more explanations or apologies about her and my useless Dad, I didn't want her 'your-problems-are-all-our-fault' routine. I was my own person and I could make my own mistakes without any help from her.

Like tonight.

I crawled into bed with my make-up still on, and fell asleep straight away. Three hours later I woke up with a throbbing head and a sore swollen throat from all that crying, but I took a couple of paracetamol and a pint of water, and told myself I'd make it up with Steph in the morning.

I'd make it up *to* Steph. She was my best friend. I knew she'd forgive me and that almost made me feel worse.

I felt so awful – not just my head and my stomach, either – I was afraid I'd never get back to sleep.

But I did.

Chapter Three

Boy, did I ever get back to sleep. Even though it was summer and the sun always rose ridiculously early, I knew as soon as I woke that I'd overslept. Groaning, I rolled onto my side and fumbled for my radio alarm. I had to knock it with the side of my hand to turn it towards me – the table was in chaos since last night, with an upturned water glass and a collapsed pile of books and CDs – but eventually I managed to focus on the blurred blue numbers.

I swore.

For a moment, I rolled on to my back, thinking: That's okay, it's Saturday, then.

No, it wasn't. I swore again and tumbled out of bed.

What was Mum thinking of? Was this her way of getting me into trouble at school, so the teachers would deal with me and she wouldn't have to? Yeah, that would be like her.

I banged the wardrobe door, flung a chair out of my way, making an unholy racket. It wasn't as if I'd be disturbing anyone: Mum would have got herself to work. Selfish cow. Tears stung my eyes. I was really in trouble now and it was her fault. All her fault.

Stumbling on something, I almost fell. My jeans, kicked off last night and left on the floor because I didn't have the hand-eye coordination to fold them over the chair. With that, the whole debacle came back to me. The repulsive Kieran. The awful walk home: how had I managed that without getting mugged, raped or run over? What a Class A clown I was.

And Steph. Falling out with Steph. This morning I could see – at least a little, through my stinging headache – how much I'd been in the wrong.

That was it. Definitely. I was going to stop drinking.

I was going to stop drinking so much, anyway. On weekdays. And I'd make my first one a lot later. I had it under control, I did, but it made me act stupid, and I wasn't stupid.

Very, very carefully I made my way

downstairs, trying not to jar my brain and stomach with every step. This hangover was a whopper. I'd have a laugh with Steph about it. Yes, that was a good idea. She'd think it was funny and say I deserved it, and I'd agree, and exaggerate my agony a bit, and be all contrite. We'd be fine again in no time. Carefully, carefully down the stairs. I felt like Winnie-the-Pooh, like my head was bumping off every step.

Another joke to tell Steph. I laughed silently, though even that made me feel queasy.

I got the shock of my life – up to that moment, at least – when I shoved open the kitchen door. Mum hadn't gone to work. She was sitting at the table, still in her dressing gown, hands clasped tightly round a mug of tea. Her head jerked up.

As she goggled at me, horror-stricken, I

realised she hadn't heard me coming. Otherwise she might have done something about the tears streaking her face, and her swollen red eyes.

I didn't know where to start.

'What's the idea, Mum?' Aggression seemed the safest policy. I hoped this wasn't going to be the lecture she'd been trying to give me for months. I wasn't in the mood right now. 'Why didn't you wake me up? Mum! I'm late!'

She opened her mouth, but all she could do was bite her lip. Tears trickled out of her eyes again. I was mortified.

'Chloe, it's okay.' Her voice was hoarse. 'I've called the school. It's fine.'

'Mum.' I glowered at her. 'Why did you call them?' It struck me. 'Is it Dad again?'

'No, it's – no. No, Chloe, it's not Dad. *Ow!*'

The mug must have burned her. She

dropped it like a hot coal and put her scalded hands over her mouth. It broke in two clean pieces, flooding the kitchen table with milky tea.

I stared at the spreading puddle. I stared at Mum.

Slowly she drew her hands down from her mouth. 'Oh, Chloe,' she said. 'Oh, Chloe. Something's happened.'

And that's when she gave me the real shock of my life.

Chapter Four

Clutching my plastic bag in one trembling
hand, I shoved open the wrought iron gates.
They creaked and groaned like something
out of a bad scary movie. Not that movies
frightened me any more: there were scarier
things in the world than special effects.
I wished I could tell Steph that. Steph used
to shriek like a banshee at the gory bits.

Steph loved scary movies.

This place looked different without all the people, all the black cars. The lawns and beds were lovely and empty and soulless, a manicured municipal garden. Except for the regimented headstones, of course. Except for those.

My heart thrashed. I desperately didn't want to be seen. I still felt like some primitive life form that hadn't been long out of the swamp, and I didn't think I was ever going to stop feeling that way.

It had been two months now, and this was the first time I'd come here since the funeral. It took me a while to find the right row, and then a little longer to find the exact place, because there wasn't a proper headstone yet. Maybe it wasn't all that hard to find; maybe deep down I just didn't want to. Maybe if I couldn't find it, it wouldn't be here, it would all have been some mad hallucination. Just a drink-fuelled nightmare.

But no. There it was. There *she* was. There was my best friend, buried in cold earth. A drink-fuelled nightmare right enough.

There was no one around, so I breathed a shaky sigh of relief and sat down cross-legged. Rummaging in my plastic bag I brought out a small potted chrysanthemum: £2.99 at the supermarket. Some of the leaves were a bit crushed, so I tweaked them ineffectually.

'I'm sorry,' I told Steph. 'It's pretty rubbish.'

I put it down on her grave anyway, and pulled my cider bottle out of the bag.

Guiltily I glanced around. If anybody saw me I'd be mortified. But there was no one, so

I twisted the bottle open, holding it away as cider foamed up out of the neck. When it settled, I filled a plastic cup, then trickled it on to the turf that covered my friend.

'There you go,' I said. 'I was reading about the Greeks. And they used to do this. And I thought you might like a drink.' I didn't feel as stupid talking out loud as I thought I would, so I tipped out another cupful for her. 'So there you go. Kiddo.'

That's when I started to cry. I hadn't meant to, it just happened. I'd cried before, of course, but not like this. I cried till I couldn't breathe, I cried till my whole body was empty.

I don't know how long I went on, but by the end of it I had a raging thirst. I looked at the bottle, and I looked at Steph's grave, and I looked at the bottle again.

'It's a bit early for me,' I told her with a

weak smile. I poured myself a half glass, though, because I really was thirsty. I took one mouthful.

'Bit early for me too, but I'll have a half,' said Rob Yeadon.

Trying to jump up, I almost fell over.

'What are you doing here?' I barked, trying to rub my eyes without making them even more bloodshot and swollen. 'You've got a nerve!'

'Oh yeah? How have I got a nerve?' His lip curled.

I wanted to hit him in the face with the cider bottle.

'You never even liked her. And she never liked you!'

'Yeah? So what?'

'So you shouldn't be here.' I called him something terrible. I told him where to go. Then a horrible thought struck me, turning my leaden stomach. 'How long have you been here?'

He shrugged.

'Just got here,' he lied. 'Minute ago.'

It was nice of him to lie, instead of mocking me. So when he sat down at my side, I didn't bite his head off, but poured him half a cup of cider instead.

'Do they know what happened yet?' he asked.

I shrugged.

'Doesn't everyone? Kieran was hammered. The car left the road and hit a tree. They say he must have been doing seventy on the corner. He's still in hospital.'

Rob examined his drink.

'It's the wrong one that died, isn't it?'

That was what I kept thinking too, so I surprised myself when I said, 'There's never a right one to die, is there?'

'Maybe not.'

At least the stupid jerk Kieran was in hospital. At least he got hurt. Not very charitable of me, but the best I could do with my furious grief. And Calum and Jenna and Ricky weren't badly hurt. At least he didn't kill them too.

What a lottery it was.

'See, it's my fault,' I said. 'Steph was all wrapped up in Calum, she didn't know how much Kieran had been drinking. I should have realised. He was sitting right beside me. Three big bottles, nearly! Should have known I couldn't get through all that by myself.'

'I wouldn't go that far,' said Rob, smiling slightly.

I gave him a sharp look, then thought: Well. I deserved that.

'She offered to walk me home,' I went on. 'I wouldn't let her. I'd kind of fallen out

46

with her.' Fiercely I rubbed my eye.

I'm fed up with you, okay? That's what I'd yelled at her. *I don't need you. I don't want your company.*

Well, I sure didn't have it now. I rubbed my whole face with the palm of my hand. It was wet. I'd thought I'd dried up my tear ducts but obviously not.

'Listen,' said Rob. 'She got in the car all by herself.'

'I know,' I said.

'She knew he'd been drinking. How would she not know? Even if she didn't know how much, she must have known he'd been drinking.'

'I told her where to go,' I said. 'I wouldn't let her come with me.'

'You've just told me where to go,' pointed out Rob. 'But if I fall down a hole on my way home it won't really be your fault.'

His logic infuriated me. Sniffing hard, I stared at the sky.

'I still feel like a piece of dirt.'

'Yeah, course. You will do.'

Which, in a funny way, made me feel better. I was up to glowering at him again.

'So why are you here?' I said belligerently.

Taking a mouthful of cider, he wrinkled his nose, and poured out the rest. Then he pointed the empty cup at a headstone two rows away.

'That's my dad,' he said.

Blood rushed to my face. I knew his dad was dead; stupid of me. He'd been dead for a few years. Rob had been at a different primary from me, so I don't know what had happened to his dad. Never liked to ask, never had the nerve. But I should have realised that's why Rob was here. Not for Steph at all.

'Sorry,' I mumbled.

'S'okay.' He balanced his plastic cup on his fingertip, catching it when it fell. 'Died of drink, y'know. Just like Steph.'

I bristled.

'Steph didn't die of—'

'Well, neither did Dad, really. He died of a number 22 bus. He was out on the lash with his mates and they were fooling around and he stepped back into the road and—' He shrugged. 'Well. Hit by the proverbial bus. How stupid is that?'

I looked at my plastic cup of cider. How stupid is that? I hadn't drunk any more of it and the urge had gone for the moment, so I trickled it back into the bottle, and stuffed the bottle back in its bag. Not knowing what to say, I stared at Rob's dad's headstone. It was black marble with a curlicued border, and an etching of roses twined round a racing car.

'That,' I said, 'is the ugliest headstone I've ever seen.'

Which just goes to prove I've got a big mouth even when I haven't been drinking.

All Rob said was, 'Yeah. Hideous, isn't it?'

We sat in companionable silence for a while. The autumn sun was warm on the back of my neck and I felt a little more peaceful now. I think all that crying had helped. I wished Steph hadn't got in the car with Kieran. I wished more than anything I'd been there to stop her.

'Sorry I kept winding you up,' said Rob, hurriedly and half under his breath.

'Yeah, that's okay,' I said.

'So do you want walking home?' he asked. 'Or are you going to tell me where to go?'

I could have said *I don't need you* or *I don't want your company*. But look what happened last time.

Besides, I didn't want to say it. I still couldn't stand him, and I decided he probably still despised me, but I didn't want to hurt his feelings, and he seemed to be trying hard to spare mine. I didn't want to go out with him. Not right now. I wasn't in a fit state to have a friend, and I probably didn't deserve one. But I'd started to hope I might not feel that way forever.

As I got to my feet I picked up my plastic bag. There was a wheelie bin right outside the cemetery gates, and this bottle would be flat before I felt like drinking it again.

'Yeah,' I said, and smiled at Rob. 'You can walk me home.'

Look out for this exciting story
in the *Shades* series:

FOUR DEGREES MORE

Malcolm Rose

Our housing estate was right at the edge of
the massive oil refinery. Not a great view
and not a nice smell for people like me, Keir
and plenty more from school. Good cover
for the Cooler, though. Peering round one
house, I checked out the road. It was quiet
and empty. But not dark. The factory's

floodlights made the place look like a football stadium in winter. But I didn't want an audience for my little game. I'd be in deep trouble if someone spotted me. I carried on creeping through the estate.

I found what I wanted about half a mile further on. Thanks to a broken light bulb or whatever, one floodlight wasn't working. Below it, the wire fence was in the dark. It wasn't completely black but that was okay because I had to see what I was doing. Hoping that any CCTV cameras wouldn't be able to make me out in the shadow, I dashed across the road and up the sloping verge. Kneeling by the fence, I grasped the wire-cutters in a sweaty right hand. I was about to snip the first diamond-shape when it struck me that the fence could be electrified.

No. Surely not. I'd never seen signs

warning people to keep their dogs and babies away.

Squeezing the handle, the cutters made a satisfying click as the wire at the bottom snapped. And I wasn't electrocuted. Far from stopping my heart, my vandalism was making it pound like crazy. Great stuff.

Another few seconds and two more snips. I reckoned I'd have to clip away for a minute before I could make a gap big enough to crawl through. I was concentrating on what I was doing but I was also listening for cars, voices or alarms going off. There was nothing.

I wasn't going to chop out a complete hole. That wouldn't have been clever. I just needed to cut enough to bend the wire back to make a door. Then, after I'd got through, I could fold it back into place. Anyone passing would've probably seen a hole but I doubted that they'd notice a slit.

When I thought I'd cut far enough up from the ground, I started going across. Only a few more snips and I'd be able to bend the netting inwards. But I wasn't quick enough.

I don't know exactly what told me – maybe a footstep or the sound of a breath – but I knew someone was behind me. Spinning round, I saw two men. They didn't look like security or police. No uniform.

The one on the right looked familiar. He whispered, 'That's not a good idea right now.'

'What?' I exclaimed.

'Keep your voice down. Come on. Come with us.'

'What?' I repeated, this time in a hush.

'Forget what you're about to do.'

'You've got to be— Who are you?'

'WHOOP.'

'What?' I said for the third time, getting up off my knees and holding the wire-cutters out like a knife.

The man sighed impatiently. 'It stands for We Have Only One Planet. We're the people who run the GreenWatch website.'

'How did you know I was—'

Interrupting, he said, 'We were protesting at the power plant when you did your bit of graffiti. Ever since, we've been ... keeping an eye on you.'

'Following me!' Lowering my voice again, I muttered, 'You're the bloke on the bike.'

'My name's Robin.' He glanced up and down the road. 'It's time to go.'

'Are you going to bundle me into the back of a car?'

Robin smiled.

'We wouldn't be very green if we went around in cars kidnapping people, would we? We just want you to come and have a chat with Beth.'

'Beth?'

He nodded.

'We admire what you're doing here, but it's just a prank really.'

'How do you know what I'm going to do?'

'Look. We're planning something much bigger and what you're doing will mess it up. There's a good time to use your hole in the fence, but it's not now. Come and talk to Beth.'

At last, the second man spoke.

'This way,' he said quietly, turning his back and making for downtown.

Look out for these other great titles in the *Shades* series:

Cuts Deep
by Catherine Johnson

Devon's heading for
trouble till he meets
Savannah, and starts to
change. But can he ever
put the past behind him?

Virus
by Mary Chapman

Penna's life is
controlled by a computer
programme. Until a
virus gets into the system
and the whole world is
under threat…

Man Trap
by Tish Farrell

Danny doesn't want to be a hunter, but the rains have failed and he and his father must go out poaching or his family will starve. Then Danny makes a fatal mistake…

Danger Money
by Mary Chapman

Bob Thompson is thrilled when he goes to work on the *Admiral*, an armed smack defending itself against German U boats. But it's not long before he really has to earn his danger money…